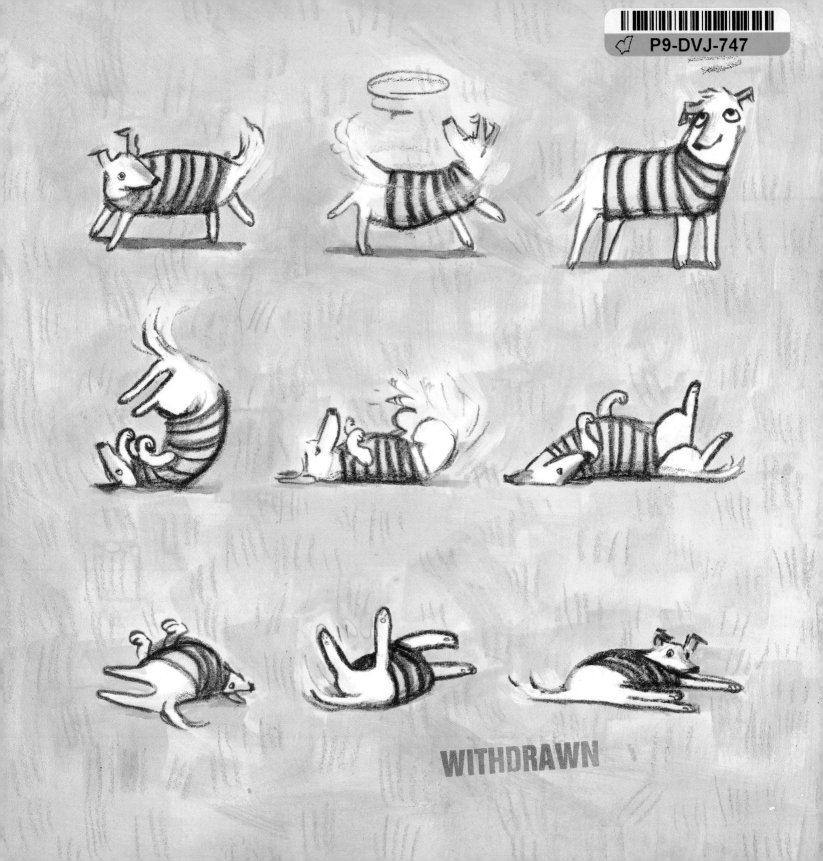

Excellent
Ed

By
Stacy McAnulty

Illustrated by
Julia Sarcone-Roach

Alfred A. Knopf New York

All the Ellis children were excellent at something.
Except Ed.

And all the Ellis children were allowed to eat at the table

and ride in the van

and sit on the couch

and use the indoor bathroom.

Except Ed.

Elaine was an excellent soccer player.

Ed preferred to carry the ball in his mouth.

The twins, Emily and Elmer, were excellent at math and could add faster than a calculator.

Ed could only count to four.

Edith was an excellent ballerina and could twirl on her toes.

Ed could twirl, too.
But it wasn't the same.

Ernie baked excellent cupcakes.

Ed agreed.

Maybe if I was excellent like Elaine, Emily, Elmer, Edith, and Ernie, then I could eat at the table and ride in the van and sit on the couch and use the indoor bathroom, **Ed thought.**

But what was Ed excellent at?

Then he got it. *Breaking stuff!*

I'm definitely excellent at breaking stuff.
Ed thought that should earn him a place at the Ellis family table.

But before he could jump onto a chair, Elaine zoomed into the kitchen and yelled, "I broke the record for most soccer goals in a season!"

Elaine was better at breaking stuff than Ed.

I must be excellent at something else, Ed thought.
Then he got it. *Losing stuff!*

MISSING
CUPCAKE

LOST
DOG
SWEATER

LOST
BALL

TRAIN

Just last week, he lost *himself* when he wandered
out of the backyard.
I'm definitely excellent at losing stuff, Ed thought.

Ed thought that earned him a ride in the van. But just as he was about to jump in, Elmer shouted, "I lost a tooth!"
"Me too!" Emily said.

MISSING
CUPCAKE

LOST
DOG

LOST
BALL

SWEATER

TRAIN

Elmer and Emily were better at losing stuff than Ed.

I must be excellent at something,
Ed thought. *Better than Elaine,
Emily, Elmer, Edith, and Ernie.*
But what?

Forgetting stuff!

He always forgot to wipe his paws. And he forgot that he shouldn't water the rosebushes. And he always seemed to forget that he had just eaten.

"Ed, you just ate!" Dad said.

I'm definitely excellent at forgetting stuff,
  Ed thought.
He was sure that earned him a nap on
  the couch, but then Edith made
  an announcement.

"I'm the new lead ballerina. When I auditioned, I just forgot to be nervous and danced my best ever."

Ed whimpered. He wasn't even the best forgetter.
Maybe I'm not excellent enough to be part of the Ellis family.

Just then, Ernie dropped half of his peanut butter
sandwich. Ed gobbled it up.
"Wow, Ed! You are excellent at cleaning the
floor," Ernie said.

Yes, I am an excellent floor cleaner.
Maybe that's why I don't eat at the table?

Then Emily and Elmer walked in the front door. Ed jumped up and
covered them with kisses.
"Ed! You're excellent at welcoming us home," Emily and Elmer said.

Yes, I am an excellent welcomer.
Maybe that's why I don't go away in the van?

Later, the family squished together on the couch, and there was
no room for Ed. So he lay across Edith's and Elaine's feet.

"Ed is excellent at warming feet,"
Elaine whispered to Edith.

Yes, I am an excellent feet warmer. Maybe
that's why I don't sit on the couch.
Ed wagged his tail. He was an Excellent
Ellis after all.

Now, if he could just figure out why
he wasn't allowed to use the
indoor bathroom . . .

For Brett —S.M.
To Paul and Lori —J.S.-R.

THIS IS A BORZOI BOOK PUBLISHED BY ALFRED A. KNOPF

Text copyright © 2016 by Stacy McAnulty

Jacket art and interior illustrations copyright © 2016 by Julia Sarcone-Roach

All rights reserved. Published in the United States by Alfred A. Knopf, an imprint of Random House
Children's Books, a division of Penguin Random House LLC, New York.

Knopf, Borzoi Books, and the colophon are registered trademarks of Penguin Random House LLC.

Visit us on the Web! randomhousekids.com

Educators and librarians, for a variety of teaching tools, visit us at RHTeachersLibrarians.com

Library of Congress Cataloging-in-Publication Data
Names: McAnulty, Stacy, author. | Sarcone-Roach, Julia, illustrator.
Title: Excellent Ed / by Stacy McAnulty ; illustrated by Julia Sarcone-Roach.
Description: First edition. | New York : Alfred A. Knopf, 2016.
Summary: Everyone in the Ellis family is excellent, except Ed the dog, who is determined to find
    something at which he, too, can excel.
Identifiers: LCCN 2015029134 | ISBN 978-0-553-51023-2 (trade) |
ISBN 978-0-553-51024-9 (lib. bdg.) | ISBN 978-0-553-51025-6 (ebook)
Subjects: | CYAC: Dogs—Fiction. | Family life—Fiction. | Ability—Fiction. | Humorous stories. | BISAC:
    JUVENILE FICTION / Animals / Dogs. | JUVENILE FICTION / Humorous Stories. | JUVENILE FICTION /
    Family / General (see also headings under Social Issues).
Classification: LCC PZ7.M47825255 Ex 2016 | DDC [E]—dc23
LC record available at http://lccn.loc.gov/2015029134

The illustrations in this book were created using acrylic paint, watercolor, crayon, and grease pencil.

MANUFACTURED IN CHINA

May 2016 10 9 8 7 6 5 4 3 2 1 First Edition

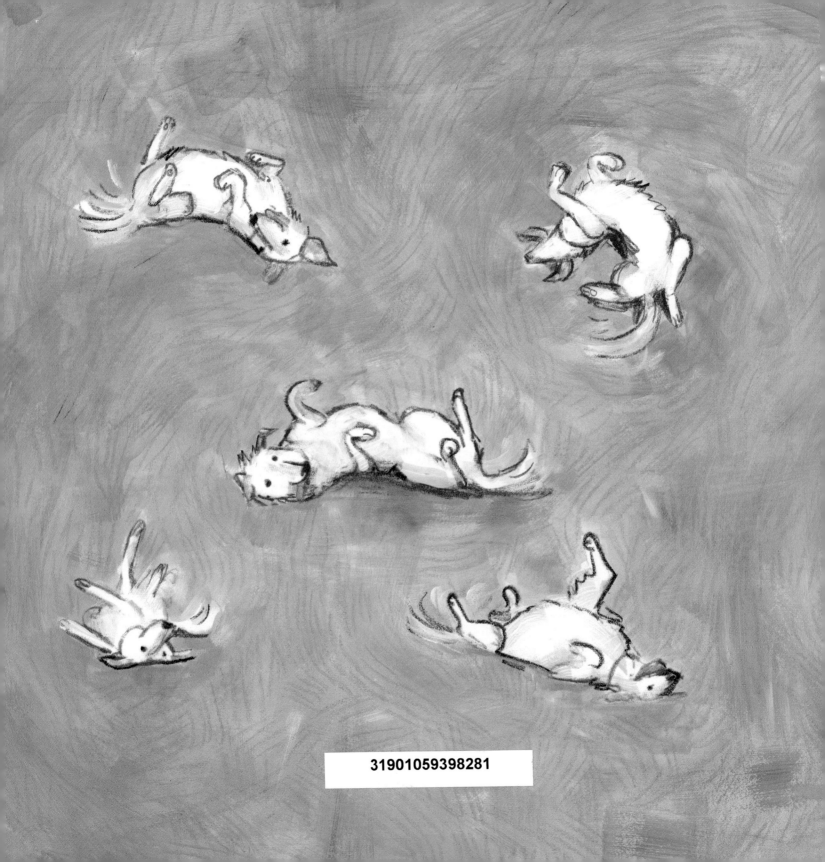